TENNESSEE VOLUNTEERS
BY
LEAH KAMINSKI
INSIDE
COLLEGE
FOOTBALL
MEDIA ENHANCED BOOKS
AV2
BY WEIGL
ADDED VALUE • AUDIO VISUAL
www.av2books.com

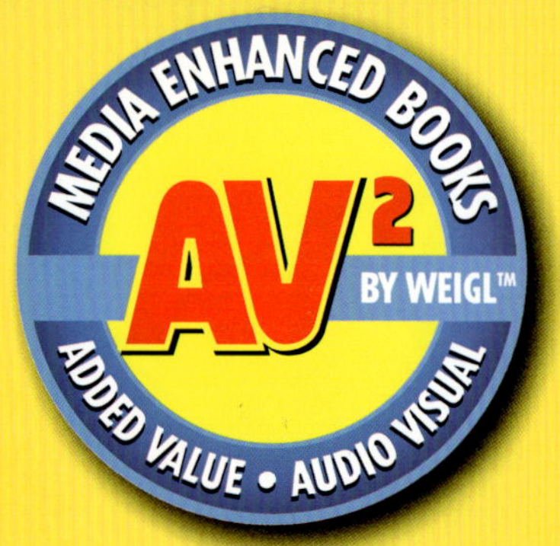

Go to **www.av2books.com**, and enter this book's unique code.

BOOK CODE

AVS97628

AV² by Weigl brings you media enhanced books that support active learning.

AV² provides enriched content that supplements and complements this book. Weigl's AV² books strive to create inspired learning and engage young minds in a total learning experience.

Your AV² Media Enhanced books come alive with...

Audio
Listen to sections of the book read aloud.

Key Words
Study vocabulary, and complete a matching word activity.

Video
Watch informative video clips.

Quizzes
Test your knowledge.

Embedded Weblinks
Gain additional information for research.

Slideshow
View images and captions, and prepare a presentation.

Try This!
Complete activities and hands-on experiments.

... and much, much more!

Published by AV² by Weigl
350 5th Avenue, 59th Floor
New York, NY 10118
Website: www.av2books.com

Library of Congress Control Number: 2018968225

ISBN 978-1-7911-0132-9 (hardcover)
ISBN 978-1-7911-0133-6 (multi-user eBook)
ISBN 978-1-7911-0134-3 (single-user eBook)

Printed in Guangzhou, China
1 2 3 4 5 6 7 8 9 0 23 22 21 20 19

042019
102318

Project Coordinator: Jared Siemens   Designer: Terry Paulhus

Every reasonable effort has been made to trace ownership and to obtain permission to reprint copyright material. The publishers would be pleased to have any errors or omissions brought to their attention so that they may be corrected in subsequent printings.

The publisher acknowledges Alamy, Getty Images, and Dreamstime as its primary image suppliers for this title.

Tennessee Volunteers

CONTENTS

Introduction

The University of Tennessee (UT) Volunteers, often called the "Vols," play in the Southeastern Conference (SEC) of the National College Athletic Association (NCAA). The Vols have a long history of incredible success. They are the last major college team to have an undefeated, untied season without allowing a single point to be scored against them. They also hold the NCAA record for shutting out opponents for 71 **consecutive** quarters. Head Coach Jeremy Pruitt gives UT the hope of more success to come.

The Volunteers are also known for many long-running **traditions**. Before each game, players run onto the field through a giant "Power T" formed by the band. The "Vol Walk" is when the team marches through surrounding streets and into Neyland Stadium, greeting fans. Fans have their own traditions, too. The Vols' stadium is located on the banks of the Tennessee River, and hundreds of fans dock their boats outside the stadium before games. These fans are known as the "Vol Navy."

Quarterback Keller Chryst transferred to the University of Tennessee as a graduate student for his final year of eligibility in 2018. He played three seasons and earned his undergraduate degree from Stanford University.

Although he signed on as a wide receiver and has practiced with the defense as a linebacker, Tennessee's Princeton Fant played as running back for the Vols during the 2018 season.

TENNESSEE

Stadium Shields-Watkins Field at Neyland Stadium

Division Southeastern Conference (SEC) Eastern

Head Coach Jeremy Pruitt

Location Knoxville, Tennessee

National Championships 3

Nicknames Volunteers, Vols, UT

3
Perfect Seasons

46
First-Round NFL Draft Picks

93
First-Team All-Americans

36
Undefeated Seasons at Home

History

The Volunteers' nickname comes from the State of Tennessee's nickname. It is called the **Volunteer State** because so many Tennessee residents stepped up for the **War of 1812** (1812–1815).

Among his many accomplishments during his years of coaching at Tennessee, Phillip Fulmer never lost a game to UT rivals the University of Kentucky Wildcats. A street near Neyland Stadium is named for Fulmer.

The Vols played their first football game in November 1891. They only played a few games each season in the early years. The team first came to greatness under General Robert R. Neyland, now a team **legend**. Neyland coached the team three different times, as he was enlisted to serve in the army in between coaching assignments. In 1927, his second season, Tennessee had an 8–0–1 record and won the Southern Conference championship. Neyland went on to lead the team to seven undefeated seasons and a National Championship in 1951.

Another important era for UT was under Coach Doug Dickey, who started in 1964. Many fans credit him with rebuilding the program. He brought the famous "T" offensive formation to UT. Dickey's record was 46–15–4 across his six seasons. He led the team to two SEC championships. More recent decades have also been successful, especially under Phillip Fulmer in the 1990s. Fulmer guided Tennessee to its third National Championship in 1998. He led some of the strongest consecutive years in team history.

Across their history, the Volunteers have won three National Championships, and they have played even more great seasons. The team has an all-time record of 833–383–53. They have won nearly 68 percent of their games.

Robert Neyland was known for his "Seven Maxims of Football," a list of seven statements that he felt summarized what it took for a team to win a game. UT players still recite them before every game.

The Stadium

Before the team takes the field at Neyland Stadium, Tennessee's marching band, the Pride of the Southland, forms the "Power T" as part of the pregame show, which concludes with "Stars and Stripes Forever."

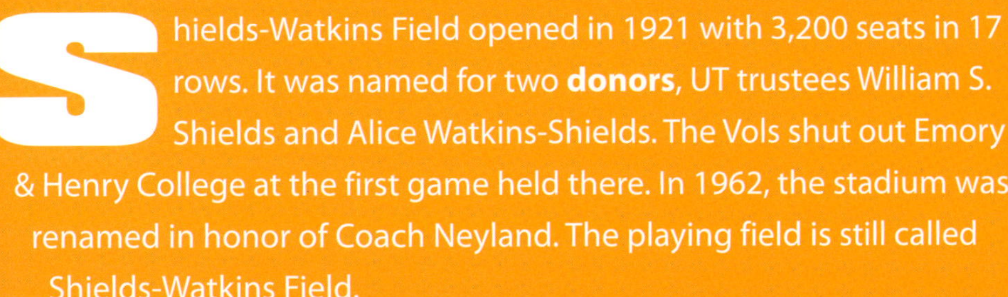

Shields-Watkins Field opened in 1921 with 3,200 seats in 17 rows. It was named for two **donors**, UT trustees William S. Shields and Alice Watkins-Shields. The Vols shut out Emory & Henry College at the first game held there. In 1962, the stadium was renamed in honor of Coach Neyland. The playing field is still called Shields-Watkins Field.

The stadium has been expanded many times over the years. It became a bowl in 1980. This means every side of the field is now surrounded by seats that create a bowl shape. The last major expansion came in 1996, when the stadium seated more than 100,000 for the first time. Its 102,455-seat capacity makes Neyland the nation's fifth-largest college stadium. Record attendance at the stadium was 109,061 at a game against the University of Florida on September 18, 2004.

The Volunteers have an all-time winning record at home of more than 460 games. This gives them an excellent winning percentage of 77.5 percent at their home venue. Tennessee has had 85 winning seasons in 96 years at Neyland Stadium. The most recent team to go undefeated at home was the 2007 team.

Neyland Stadium's Jumbotron scoreboard, installed in 2009, measures 124 feet (38 meters) wide by 37 feet (11 m) high. There are permanent images on the back of the board featuring former UT players Al Wilson and Jason Witten, and legendary UT coach Robert Neyland.

Where They Play

Welcome to Shields-Watkins Field at Neyland Stadium, home of the University of Tennessee Volunteers. The stadium stands are a sea of orange and white on game days, as nearly 100,000 fans fill the seats. The marching band forms the famous "Power T" as the team takes the field. Fans and alumni love gathering in Neyland Stadium to watch the Vols win.

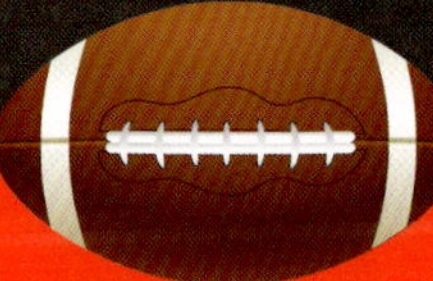

SEC WEST

1. **Auburn University**
   Auburn, Alabama
2. **Louisiana State University**
   Baton Rouge, Louisiana
3. **Mississippi State University**
   Starkville, Mississippi
4. **Texas A&M University**
   College Station, Texas
5. **University of Alabama**
   Tuscaloosa, Alabama
6. **University of Arkansas**
   Fayetteville, Arkansas
7. **University of Mississippi**
   Oxford, Mississippi

Arena
Shields-Watkins Field at Neyland Stadium

Location
Knoxville, Tennessee

Broke Ground
March 21, 1921

Completed
September 24, 1921

Surface
Real Grass

Features
- Located on the banks of the Tennessee River
- Home to one of college football's largest LED displays, with a price tag exceeding $4 million
- Distinctive orange-and-white checkerboard design in both end zones since 1964

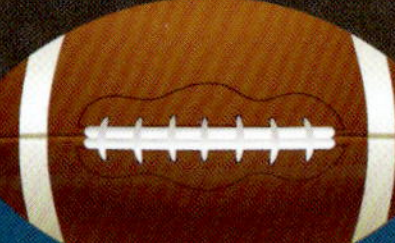

SEC EAST

1. **University of Florida**
   Gainesville, Florida
2. **University of Georgia**
   Athens, Georgia
3. **University of Kentucky**
   Lexington, Kentucky
4. **University of Missouri**
   Columbia, Missouri
5. **University of South Carolina**
   Columbia, South Carolina
6. ★ **University of Tennessee**
   Knoxville, Tennessee
7. **Vanderbilt University**
   Nashville, Tennessee

NEW HAMPSHIRE
MAINE
VERMONT
MASSACHUSETTS
RHODE ISLAND
NEW YORK
CONNECTICUT
NEW JERSEY
DELAWARE
MARYLAND
WASHINGTON, D.C.
PENNSYLVANIA
NORTH DAKOTA
SOUTH DAKOTA
MINNESOTA
WISCONSIN
MICHIGAN
IOWA
NEBRASKA
ILLINOIS
INDIANA
OHIO
WEST VIRGINIA
VIRGINIA
KENTUCKY
KANSAS
MISSOURI
NORTH CAROLINA
TENNESSEE
SOUTH CAROLINA
OKLAHOMA
ARKANSAS
MISSISSIPPI
ALABAMA
GEORGIA
TEXAS
LOUISIANA
FLORIDA
Atlantic Ocean
Gulf of Mexico
LEGEND
Home Stadium
SEC West
SEC East
United States
Other Countries
Water
SCALE
0 miles
500 miles
0 kilometers
500 km

The Uniforms

During the second half of the 1965 season, the Vols added a **black cross** to the middle of the "Power T" **in memory** of three assistant coaches who died in a car accident that October.

In 2009, the Volunteers wore black jerseys with orange pants for a night game on Halloween.

The University of Tennessee's colors are orange and white. The orange color comes from the color of the American daisy that grows on campus. Team members wear white pants and white helmets, with orange jerseys at home and white jerseys away. Players also wear eye-catching alternate uniforms. Black was the team's primary uniform color in the early 1900s, and in recent years, the team's regular alternate jersey was dark gray, but new coach Jeremy Pruitt opted for the traditional orange and white when he took over in 2018.

AWAY

Checkerboard striping on the pants and helmets was added in 2015. It matches the field's checkerboard end zones. In 2018, the Vols wore **throwbacks** to their 1998 uniforms for the 20th anniversary of the team's National Championship season. The uniforms were white with no stripes, and the helmets had a solid orange stripe.

The helmets have not changed much since 1964. They are still white with an orange "T" decal and orange stripe down the center.

The "Power T" first appeared on Tennessee's helmets in 1964.

Student Athletes

In the days before **television**, playing in New York City was one great way for student athletes to get **noticed** by the sportswriters who choose All-American teams.

Defensive lineman Kyle Phillips was a four-time SEC Academic Honor Roll student. Phillips maintained a 3.0 grade point average (GPA) or higher during each season he played at Tennessee, from 2015 to 2018.

Being a college student athlete is hard work. Student athletes have to perform well on the football field and in the classroom. UT football players have stricter requirements than athletes in other sports. They are required to pass at least 9 of 12 credit hours per term. Tennessee student athletes have access to the Thornton Athletics Student Life Center, which offers tutoring and mentoring. UT offers many other services to help players balance the student athlete life.

Many student athletes are given athletic scholarships. An athletic scholarship is a financial aid agreement between the athlete and the college or university. Athletes who do not receive an athletic scholarship can also be "walk-on" members of the team. This means they are on the team, but without athletic financial aid. The University of Tennessee typically awards the maximum number of football scholarships allowed, which is 85.

The Thornton Athletic Student Life Center offers multiple enrichment programs for football players such as Darrin Kirkland Jr., including a career development program and a leadership academy.

Bowl Games

The NCAA records UT's first bowl game as the 1939 **Orange Bowl**. However, during the **Great Depression**, the Vols played an unofficial Charity Bowl at Yankee Stadium in 1931.

The Volunteers outscored the University of Iowa Hawkeyes by 28 points in the first half of the 2015 TaxSlayer Bowl. Tennessee went on to defeat Iowa 45–28, and UT quarterback Joshua Dobbs was named the bowl's Most Valuable Player (MVP).

After the college football season ends, a rare sports tradition begins. There is no NCAA-sponsored **postseason** for teams such as UT, who are in the Football Bowl Subdivision (FBS). Instead, a variety of games called bowl games are played. There are currently 40 bowl games. Playing in a bowl game is a chance to compete for respect and wins against rivals and new teams. For the top teams, the bowls are also a chance to compete for finalist slots in the FBS-sponsored College Football Playoff National Championship Game that now determines national champions.

The Volunteers have a successful bowl history. They rank sixth in college football history for bowl game appearances, with 52, and seventh in bowl wins, with 28. They attended 16 consecutive bowls from 1989 to 2004. The 1999 Fiesta Bowl win against the Florida State University Seminoles in the 1998 season was the **inaugural** BCS National Championship Game, and the only time UT's national title was won in a bowl game.

With a 38–24 win against the University of Nebraska Cornhuskers, the Volunteers claimed the Music City Bowl in 2016. During the game, defensive end Derek Barnett broke Vols legend Reggie White's record, with 33 career sacks.

The Coaches

Jeremy Pruitt has worked under some of college football's most successful and influential coaches. Pruitt was an assistant to Nick Saban at the University of Alabama, as well as a defensive coordinator and defensive backs coach under Jimbo Fisher at Florida State.

The Volunteers have had 26 head coaches. UT's first coach was J. A. Pierce in 1899. The current head coach is Jeremy Pruitt. John Barnhill has the highest winning percentage of Tennessee coaches who have coached more than one game, winning nearly 85 percent of his games. Five Vols coaches are in the College Football **Hall of Fame**. They are Robert Neyland, Bowden Wyatt, Doug Dickey, Johnny Majors, and Phillip Fulmer.

ROBERT NEYLAND Robert Neyland is the most **dominant** coach in Vol's history. He is the all-time Tennessee leader in games won, with 173 victories across his three coaching runs from 1926 to 1934, 1936 to 1940, and 1946 to 1952. Neyland led the team to two National Championships. He coached a streak of 33 undefeated games and a perfect season. These rare accomplishments make him a Vols legend.

PHILLIP FULMER Phillip Fulmer is a lifelong Vol. He went from football co-captain, to head coach, to UT athletic director. From 1992 to 2008, he challenged and motivated his players, including 19 first-round NFL draft picks such as Peyton Manning and Jason Witten. He won 152 games, the second-most of any UT coach. Fulmer was named National Coach of the Year and is in the College Football Hall of Fame.

JEREMY PRUITT Jeremy Pruitt is a top recruiter with a great defensive mind. Before becoming UT head coach in 2017, Pruitt was defensive coordinator for some of the best teams in the country. He coached the nation's top defense at Florida State and has overseen 13 first-round draft picks. In 2018, his first season coaching the Vols led to an improved record over the previous year.

The Mascot

During the week, Smokey X lives with a local Knoxville family. On weekends, when he has mascot duties, he lives with and is cared for by members of UT's Alpha Gamma Rho fraternity.

Smokey, a bluetick coonhound, is the Volunteers' mascot. The mascot was chosen by student vote in 1953. At halftime of that season's game against the Mississippi State University Bulldogs, several dogs were lined up. Smokey barked when introduced, so the students cheered. He barked again. They cheered louder. After this back-and-forth, Smokey was a clear favorite.

There has been a Smokey on the team ever since, provided by the same Tennessee family. Smokey leads the Vols out of the "T" at home games. Smokey VI had **heat exhaustion** from the 140° Fahrenheit (60° Celsius) temperatures on the field at a 1991 UCLA game. He was listed on the Vols injury report until he returned. Smokey VIII was the winningest Smokey, with a record of 91–22 and the 1998 National Championship. Smokey X is the current mascot.

A costumed Smokey mascot, modeled after the live version of the dog, is a regular competitor in mascot competitions and has appeared in several television commercials. Smokey was inducted into the Mascot Hall of Fame in 2008. He wears a 00 jersey and interacts with fans before and during football games.

Legends of the Past

For many players, their time with the Volunteers is the start of a promising football career. These are some of the best-known football players to play for the University of Tennessee.

Doug Atkins

Doug Atkins is among the greatest defensive linemen to ever play for UT. Very tall and strong, he was a basketball player at UT before Coach Neyland discovered him in 1950. With Atkins on defense, the Vols had a record of 29–4–1. He was named an All-American in 1952. Atkins was a first-round draft pick in 1953 by the Cleveland Browns. He went on to spend 12 seasons with the Chicago Bears. He was an eight-time Pro Bowl starter, and the 1958 Pro Bowl MVP. Atkins was the first Tennessee player to be voted into both the College Football Hall of Fame and the Pro Football Hall of Fame.

Position: Defensive End
Seasons: 1950–1952 (Tennessee Volunteers), 1953–1954 (Cleveland Browns), 1955–1966 (Chicago Bears), 1967–1969 (New Orleans Saints)
Born: May 8, 1930, Humboldt, Tennessee

Reggie White

Reggie White may have been the greatest defensive end in football history. He was called the "Minister of Defense" because he became a minister while at UT. White went unnoticed until his senior year, when he made 100 tackles and set a still-standing school record of 15 single-season sacks. He was named a consensus All-American. White was drafted by the Philadelphia Eagles and later played for the Green Bay Packers and the Carolina Panthers. During his NFL career, he was a two-time NFL Defensive Player of the Year and a 1998 **Super Bowl** winner. He has the second-most all-time sacks in the NFL and is a member of both the College and Pro Football Halls of Fame.

Position: Defensive Tackle
Seasons: 1980–1983 (Tennessee Volunteers), 1985–1992 (Philadelphia Eagles), 1993–1998 (Green Bay Packers), 2000 (Carolina Panthers)
Born: December 19, 1961, Chattanooga, Tennessee

Peyton Manning

Peyton Manning is one of the greatest quarterbacks of all time. Manning finished his UT career with 42 NCAA, SEC, and UT records. In his senior year, he won the Maxwell Award for the best college player in the nation. Manning was drafted by the Indianapolis Colts first overall in the 1998 draft. He won two NFL conference titles and one Super Bowl with the Colts. In Manning's final season, he won a second Super Bowl with the Denver Broncos and became the oldest quarterback to start and win a Super Bowl. His brother, Eli Manning, is also a legendary quarterback.

Position: Quarterback
Seasons: 1994–1997 (Tennessee Volunteers), 1998–2010 (Indianapolis Colts), 2012–2015 (Denver Broncos)
Born: March 24, 1976, New Orleans, Louisiana

Jason Witten

Jason Witten became a star in his junior year at Tennessee. He set the single-season UT record for catches, with 39, and for receiving yards by a tight end, with 493. He is known for catching the game-winning 25-yard touchdown in a historic six-overtime Vols victory against the University of Arkansas in 2002. Witten went on to become one of the greatest players in Dallas Cowboys history and one of the most dominant tight ends in the NFL. He holds the NFL record for most catches by a tight end in a game, with 18 catches on October 28, 2012. Witten retired from the NFL in 2017 and is now an ESPN TV commentator.

Position: Tight End
Seasons: 2000–2002 (Tennessee Volunteers), 2003–2017 (Dallas Cowboys)
Born: May 6, 1982, Elizabethton, Tennessee

All-Time Records

13

Most Overtime Wins

The Volunteers have the most overtime wins in NCAA history, with a 13–7 record.

1.05

Lowest Rate of Interceptions

Peyton Manning holds the SEC record for lowest percentage of interceptions, with 1.05 percent (4 interceptions in 380 passes) in 1995.

15

Single-Season Sacks

Reggie White has the UT record for most sacks in a season, with 15 in 1983.

23

Most Consecutive Pass Completions

The 1998 Vols team holds the SEC record for most consecutive completions in a game, with 23 completions against the South Carolina Gamecocks.

16

Most Consecutive Rushes

William Howard holds the NCAA record for most consecutive rushes by the same player in one game, with 16 against the University of Mississippi Ole Miss Rebels on November 15, 1986.

Timeline

Throughout the team's history, the Tennessee Volunteers have had many memorable events that have become defining moments for the team and its fans.

1891
The Vols play their first game against Sewanee, who win 24–0. The Vols do not win a game until 1892.

1921
Neyland Stadium is built. It is originally called Shields-Watkins Field.

1926
Coach Neyland is hired for his first of three stretches as head coach.

1900 1920 1940 1960

The 1926 season begins a 33-game undefeated streak that ends in 1930.

1939
The Volunteers shut out 10 consecutive opponents. No collegiate team has shut out an entire regular season since.

1953
The first Smokey is selected as the Volunteers' mascot.

1970
After the 1969 season, Coach Dickey leaves, and 28-year-old Bill Battle becomes the coach. The Vols finish 11–1 and Battle becomes the first Division I head coach to win 11 games in his first year.

1998
The Vols win their third and most recent National Championship.

The Future
The Volunteers are a team on the rise. With Coach Pruitt leading the team, the University of Tennessee defeated the highly ranked Kentucky Wildcats and Auburn University Tigers in 2018. Since 1902, the team has earned 814 total wins, 13 conference championships, and 3 National Championships. The Vols hope to carry their legacy of winning into future seasons.

2017
Jeremy Pruitt is hired as head coach.

1980

2000

2020

1983
Led by Reggie White, the Volunteers end a difficult decade. They finish a 9–3 season by winning the Florida Citrus Bowl.

1992
Phillip Fulmer is named head coach.

In 2016, the Vols win their third consecutive bowl game.

Write a Biography

Life Story

A person's life story can be the subject of a book. This kind of book is called a biography. Biographies often describe the lives of people who have achieved great success. These people may be alive today, or they may have lived many years ago. Reading a biography can help you learn more about a great person.

Get the Facts

Use this book, and research in the library and on the internet, to find out more about your favorite player. Learn as much about him as you can. What position does he play? What are his statistics in important categories? Has he set any records? Also, be sure to write down key events in the person's life. What was his childhood like? What has he accomplished off the field? Is there anything else that makes this person special or unusual?

Use the Concept Web

A concept web is a useful research tool. Read the questions in the concept web on the following page. Answer the questions in your notebook. Your answers will help you write a biography.

Concept Web

Adulthood
- Where does this individual currently reside?
- Does he have a family?

Your Opinion
- What did you learn from the books you read in your research?
- Would you suggest these books to others?
- Was anything missing from these books?

Accomplishments off the Field
- What is this person's life's work?
- Has he received awards or recognition for accomplishments?
- How have this person's accomplishments served others?

Childhood
- Where and when was this person born?
- Describe his parents, siblings, and friends.
- Did he grow up in unusual circumstances?

Write a Biography

Help and Obstacles
- Did this individual have a positive attitude?
- Did he receive help from others?
- Did this person have a mentor?
- Did this person face any hardships?
- If so, how were the hardships overcome?

Accomplishments on the Field
- What records does this person hold?
- What key games and plays have defined his career?
- What are his stats in categories important to his position?

Work and Preparation
- What was this person's education?
- What was his work experience?
- How does this person work?
- What is the process he uses?

Trivia Time

Take this quiz to test your knowledge of the Tennessee Volunteers. The answers are printed upside down under each question.

1 In which conference do the Volunteers play?

A. The SEC

2 What is the team's entrance into the stadium called?

A. The "Vol Walk"

3 How many National Championships have the Volunteers won?

A. Three

4 Which head coach led the team three different times?

A. General Robert Neyland

5 What design is painted on the end zones at Neyland Stadium?

A. A checkerboard

6 What is the logo on the UT helmet called?

A. The "Power T"

7 Which team did the Volunteers defeat to win the National Championship for the 1998 season?

A. The Florida State Seminoles

8 What kind of dog is Smokey?

A. A bluetick coonhound

9 Which UT player was called the "Minister of Defense"?

A. Reggie White

10 Which former Vol quarterback has a brother who is also a famous quarterback?

A. Peyton Manning

Key Words

consecutive: following in an unbroken order

dominant: more powerful or influential than others

donors: people who give something, usually money to pay for a building, item, or service

Hall of Fame: a group of persons judged to be outstanding in a particular sport

heat exhaustion: a result of the body overheating that may include heavy sweating and a rapid pulse

inaugural: the first in a series of similar events

legend: an extremely well-known or famous person

postseason: a sporting event that takes place after the end of the regular season

Super Bowl: the NFL's annual championship game between the winning team from the National Football Conference and the winning team from the American Football Conference

throwbacks: new items that borrow characteristics from earlier editions

traditions: customs or beliefs that are passed from one generation to another

Index

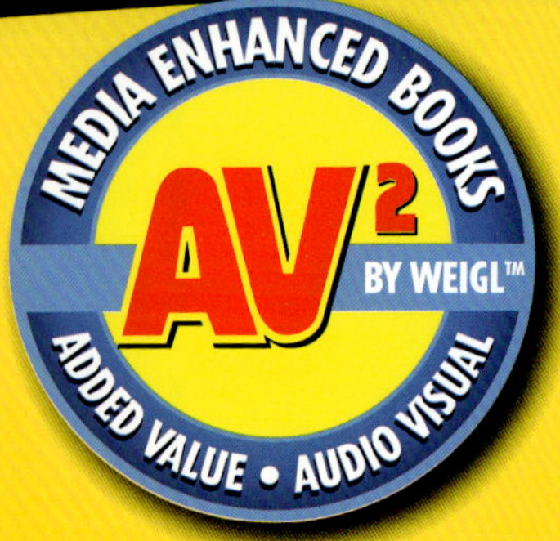

Log on to www.av2books.com

AV² by Weigl brings you media enhanced books that support active learning. Go to www.av2books.com, and enter the special code found on page 2 of this book. You will gain access to enriched and enhanced content that supplements and complements this book. Content includes video, audio, weblinks, quizzes, a slideshow, and activities.

AV² Online Navigation

Book Pages
AV² pages directly correspond to pages in the book.

Audio
Listen to sections of the book read aloud.

Video
Watch informative video clips.

Embedded Weblinks
Gain additional information for research.

Key Words
Study vocabulary, and complete a matching word activity.

Try This!
Complete activities and hands-on experiments.

Quizzes
Test your knowledge.

Slideshow
View images and captions, and prepare a presentation.

AV² was built to bridge the gap between print and digital. We encourage you to tell us what you like and what you want to see in the future.

Sign up to be an AV² Ambassador at www.av2books.com/ambassador.

Due to the dynamic nature of the internet, some of the URLs and activities provided as part of AV² by Weigl may have changed or ceased to exist. AV² by Weigl accepts no responsibility for any such changes. All media enhanced books are regularly monitored to update addresses and sites in a timely manner. Contact AV² by Weigl at 1-866-649-3445 or av2books@weigl.com with any questions, comments, or feedback.